# THE ADVENTURE

SYMBOLISM

WILLIAM HATFIELD

ISBN:978-1-990362-23-1

# ACKNOWLEDGEMENTS

I would like to thank all those who are not satisfied with the status quo of religion. The promises of something good and wonderful but never fulfilling the promise. THE ADVENTURE OF SEEKING FOR SOMETHING GREATER THAN RELIGION IS AT THE HEART OF MAN.

This is my attempt to put the globalism that is taking shape in the earth today in a science fiction format to help people become aware of the communist agendas and control of the population of the world that nations have when they begin to flow with globalism agendas.

# PROLOGUE

Have you ever woken up and thought life has to be different than what I am living! There is so much confusion and uncertainty in the earth, and it seems to be established by those in charge of our politics, religion, and financial institutions. Everyone seems to be looking for dominance and fame. What is up with people, why are we like the people who just mindlessly follow the status quo without questions?  THE NAMES IN THIS BOOK ARE NOT REFLECTION UPON ANYONE ON EARTH BUT ARE MADE UP.

# TABLE OF CONTENTS

# THE SYMBOL

I woke up that chilly winter morning to a frigid minus thirty-three Celsius and noticed friends further north complaining of minus fifty-seven Celsius with the wind chill. Every morning had become much more repetitive than I hoped for.

This worldwide pandemic has locked the earth down. Not leaving your home unless life is absolutely in jeopardy. Then you must adorn the hazmat suit supplied by government agents. This has been going on for three years. If you dare to venture outdoors, you are risking getting caught by the government-conditioned agents that patrol each neighborhood. These agents are really released criminals on death row who agreed to be the army of domination as each government of each nation seeks to enslave their citizens.

I was sitting in my easy boy chair, staring out my big picture window thinking I am glad I have nowhere to go, thus the journey from a warm house to a cold vehicle. I noticed three vehicles pulling up in front of my house covered in decals. Six men in uniform excited the vehicles and huddled together discussing a topic and looking at my house. I watched as the leader of these agents pointed in different directions and begin to give orders to the other agents. The agents saluted the leader then acted. I was always curious about the government agents as they seemed to be mindless clones walking in obedience. The men separated into two groups of three and one group approached my front door while the other group proceeded to the side of the house apparently to go to my back door. I thought I would have some fun and ignore the ringing then knocking on my front door. I went to the back door, opened it and three men were waiting for me with a rather stern look on their face.

The spokesperson for the group said, "we thought you might try to run.

Mr. Roberts you must come with us." I was allowed to get my parka as it was too cold to be outside without warm clothing. I locked my house and followed the agents to their vehicle. Two agents behind me and one in front of me.

Upon entering the S.U.V I was blindfolded and ordered to sit still and relax and all would be explained once we got to our destination. I could sense the condition of the roads we traveled. Rough and the sound of gravel soon was noticed after an hour of smooth pavement traveling. We traveled for two hours on the gravel road then turned left on a smooth road and after four hours of winding and occasional bumps turned right into what I thought was a driveway.

Exiting the S.U.V. I was roughly escorted into a building and into an elevator which proceeded to take us to lower levels. I was further escorted to a laboratory where the blind fold was removed. I chuckled at my surroundings as I had been in this place before. I chuckled because of the drama the agents always partook of. The drama was put on for public viewing and media projection of the propaganda of governments to show the citizens of the world the consequences of disobedience.

They could not be honest and just say they wanted to have a conversation with me. Always project the propaganda the government needed to control the population.

The governments of the earth had a plan and an agenda to see their goals fulfilled by a one world order including money and religion which were the most powerful forces on this planet at this time in our history. If you could  control the financial condition and religious beliefs of humanity you can control, dominate, and manipulate all humanity to do your bidding whether good or evil.

But regardless of the drama and plans, I knew I was in the government decryption Centre where they needed my help. I was always fascinated by numbers, symbols, colors, puzzles, and riddles that say one thing but have hidden meanings and purposes.

Their archeologists discovered a metal plaque with a symbol that the institute decryptions experts could only decipher so far then were stumped.

The part that they figured out startled them because it spoke of a person who was to arrive to the earth and destroy their plans and goals and establish His purposes. They wanted my help to discover the hidden meaning of the symbol so if it were more than a fantasy, they could prevent it from being fulfilled. The problem with control and domination is fear on every side.

The controlled fear the consequences of disobedience and the controllers fear rebellion and losing their control, which gives them a sense of superiority for a while. To lose it they become equal to all others, and that is not acceptable.

This symbol was shrouded in mystery.

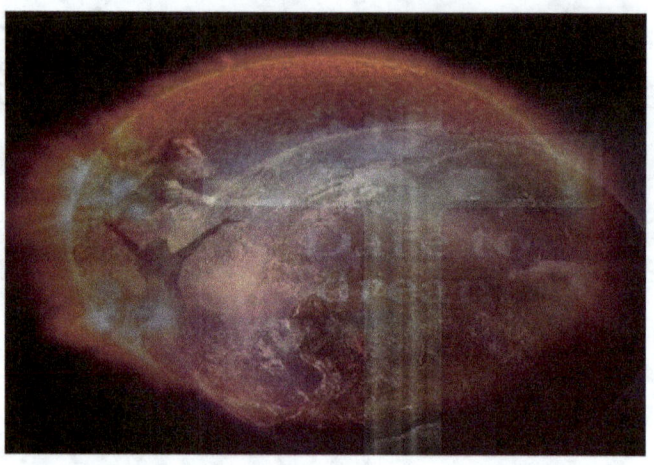

This symbol was multiple pictures overlayed with a written message. This the government could see but the merger of the pictures blurred the message that it had the potential to wake civilization to a message that could empower a rebellion of citizens against the world order being established on the earth.

In order to view the message properly the source of each picture had to be discovered so as to extract each image exactly and separately slowly revealing the message.

As I viewed the symbol embedded on the iron plate I could see some images clearly, but others had to really look and concentrate to view them. The problem is what does each image represent according to the collage of all images present which in itself gives an eternal message.

Those who are  in control do not like shadows and uncertainty unless they are the promoters of such. There are many riddles, stories, and mysteries  that are hidden for us in order for those who think they are in charge will be revealed as puppets to a master deceiver that pulls strings connected to emotional behavior and high minded personal in the earth. I slowly turned my attention from the symbolic iron to the figure who was approaching me. I have talked with many government officials and Mr. Jack Roberts is known in the academic circles as a mystery solver that nothing eventually will be outside his grasp of understanding.

I was amused as I heard the president of the earth Sabastian Hicks speak, "welcome Mr. Roberts I am pleased you showed up. I want to ask for your help because this puzzling image has me concerned!" I always spoke honorably to those in leadership regardless of my belief in their plans and agendas.

"Yes, Mr. President how can I be of assistance?" "My decryptions experts cannot figure the symbolism out on that plaque; they discovered four pictures merged together with a message written and partially covered.

After that they cannot understand the symbolism and since your specialty in life is understanding mysteries and symbols I am asking for your help in understanding this because I have an overwhelming sensation this symbol may affect my world presidency!" The world president Sabastian Hicks, voice was nervous and troubled as he made his request.

I quickly agreed to help him in his venture knowing that my refusal would cause a total transformation from the peaceful charismatic person standing before me  to an outraged egomaniac that would use violence to get his way.

There are many aspects of the world president that most citizens had no clue about. To the citizens of the earth, he came across as charismatic, kind, and concerned about their financial needs. To the inner circle he showed his manipulative domineering self-worship side and any who thought outside his box could face the guillotine and have their heads removed from their bodies.

If you want to keep your head, then go along with his self-delusions and bid your time. Even though the public adored him, his control of world governments was weak and getting weaker with each new policy he was instating on the earth. Rebellious groups were popping up around the earth regularly and quickly.

# THE PREPARATION

I had agreed to take on an adventure more by force than volunteer, but regardless the potential message seemed life altering. My training in eastern, Roman, Greek, Egyptian mythology and folklore would come in handy. I was also trained in Christian ideology in prophetic events and pre-Adamic earth history. The pre-Adamic earth idea was the earth was home to another species before man inhabited it. The theory is we are under the influence of pre-Adamic earth inhabitancy without realizing it. This theory also suggests there are portals on the earth that allow the inhabitants of this pre-Adamic earth access to the realm of existence we are living in.

I am not a religious man at heart but a science archaeologist that loves mysteries and solving them.

One of the areas I may investigate is the V.A.T.T. which stands for Vatican Advanced Technology Telescope. This telescope sits on Mount Graham. It has been rumored that there is a portal in that area where strange green reptilian-like creatures have come out of and after a time frame has gone back into it.

The reason I studied religious mythology is they are notorious for making idols, plaques, scrolls, and many more items putting value on them by declaring the fall from the heavens or brought to them from other dimensions and claiming the possessor of such items will yield unspeakable power. I personally do not believe in anything science cannot prove but the president of earth does and is in a frenzy to find as many as these artifacts as possible to have complete power, authority, and dominance over the entire earth. Even though it was given him by governments, religions, and financial institutes it was never given him by all civilians.

The growth of those deciding to not yield to the world president has grown to affect nations and religions who in the past have spoken of world domination in their belief systems.

The confidence in the one world president has reached an all-time low as his policies seem to serve his agenda and delusional ego of being greater than all humankind, gods, or anything in existence. Shortly after I left his presence to prepare for this adventure newspaper and social media and online news programs all declared that the world president declared himself to be the greatest being in existence and must be worshipped by all peoples regardless of nationalities and creeds and cultures in the earth. Glad I left when I did. Little did I realize the world president Sebastian Hicks declaration would work to my advantage in my search to figure out the symbols on the plaque and where it originated from.

Sebastian, the world president allowed me to take an imprint of the symbol on the metal plaque so it would help me in my search. As I studied the imprint closely, I realized I would probably need the help of a close friend that has been an excellent asset on other adventures. Natasha Shranko a gorgeous five'6" brunette from Estonian who has been trained in multiple martial arts studies and if you try fighting her you will  be on the ground shortly.

I know I tried jokingly to mess with her and before I could catch my breath my face was planted in a sink full of dirty dishwater. Needless to say, she made an impact on my life that merged her into a large part of my heart and emotions. The kind of thinking can I be with her on a more permanent basis rather than on occasional adventures? Regardless of old feelings I have to try and find where she is located so I can chat with her.

I decided to start my investigation on the internet by doing a search for archaeological discoveries where she would probably eventually end up.

Knowing her desire for treasure of different sorts like gold to knowledge I discovered an interesting discovery in Bukidnon, Philippines. This area in southern Philippines has been the search of many legends that promise treasures of many forms from Spanish gold to scrolls of ancient languages that share secrets of the universe's beginnings and so on.

I updated my passport and applied for a research visa to hopefully run into Natasha. Boarding the plane was uneventful. I settled in my aisle seat getting relaxed for a long flight.

I noticed a shift change happening among the flight attendants. One flight attendant who was leaving noticed me and made her way to my seat and quickly bent down and whispered in my ear, "be careful, what you are looking for has many obstacles and bad people looking for the same thing." Before I could respond she quickly left the plane, and the door was closed, and an announcement was made to put seat belts on and prepare for take-off. Settling in for the flight, I started to meditate on my mission. How did the flight attendant know what I was searching for? What parts of the globe am I going to find myself and bad men looking for the same thing? I do not even know what I am looking for. The only thing I knew was something to help understand the metal plaque with the symbol on it.

Oh well I decided to relax enjoy the flight, not rack my brain, and trust clues will present themselves when I get to the Philippines. closed my eyes for a quick nap and realize the flight attendant was gently shaking me. "Sir we have arrived and are departing the plane please grab your carry-ons and exit at the front of the plane."

As I left the plane, I noticed something rather extraordinary, people were looking in my direction and whispering amongst themselves. Curious, I went to the men's room and looked in the mirror thinking maybe someone drew a picture on my face while I slept on the plane. Noticing nothing I just put the stares and whispers down to my reputation as a scientific adventurer proceeded me. Leaving the airport, I grabbed a cab to the nearest hotel and decided to book a week to stay.

The room gave me a view over the city to the mountains above Malaybalay. Malaybalay City: A sanctuary of cool, clear mountain air. Malaybalay City is set among the Kitanglad Mountain Ranges of Bukidnon Province on the island of Mindanao. Noted as "The South Summer Home of the Philippines," the beauty of this little city is stunning.

As evening was setting in time to sit in the hotel and hook up to the Wi-Fi and see if I can find anything previously posted on the internet. Many archaeologists post daily if not hourly updates to find that it excites them. Located sixty miles south of Cagayan de Oro City, many travelling between Davao and CDO enjoy a stopover here. Valencia, a neighboring city to the south, is another perfect stopover but Malaybalay has the coolness that so many of us seek out.

The original inhabitants of Malaybalay were from the northern regions of Mindanao. They fled inland from the coastal waters filled with Moro-Muslim pirates and colonizing Spaniards. The beauty of Malaybalay for many is the cool, crisp air and the morning fog that often shrouds the city from the sun.

Many have made their way to this unique little city as a base to explore the nearby mountains, trails, parks, and paths. The Kitanglad Mountain Range has some of the tallest mountains and plunging ravines in all of Mindanao – many seldom visited, if at all.

Mount Capistrano is one of the more trekked and photographed mountains in the area. Once you see it, you will know why it has adorned the covers of numerous travel magazines around the globe. This was my first pamphlet I read on the area and decided to book two weeks as it may take me a bit of time to research and investigate the area to find clues.

I could not ignore gossip or legends or even fantasy stories people supposedly make up like bigfoot abominable snowmen, even giants that come through portals and return after a few hours because this realm is not friendly to such creatures. Time to rest tonight as tomorrow would be spent asking questions especially to older people who are more aware of legends and ancient folklore than younger people who have smart phones attached to their hands and faces buried in them. Definitely a tool to condition the mind for control and manipulation.

## NATASHA SHRANKO

I started querying people about legends folklore and even tall tales handed down from previous generations. After what seemed like hundreds of people, I came across an interesting theory about the earthquakes that happen in the Philippines. Even though the Philippines is located in the area known as "The Pacific Ring of Fire." There are several locations in the Philippines that are more prone to earthquakes than others, however, there are small earthquakes, ones which are not even noticed, somewhere in the Philippines almost daily.

Superstitious people have different theories than scientific facts. The theory I found interesting only because of the symbol I was trying to track down which has no scientific roots that I could discover was dealing with two entities.

THE ANCIENT ONE

# THE ADVERSARY

Each of these individuals was in a war with the other and when their armies clashed that would cause the earth to quake and shake. The stronger the earth quaked the bigger and longer each battle raged. The scientific facts were obviously different but for symbolic sake I thought I might explore this avenue.

Laying down for a quick nap I was disturbed by a hard knocking on the hotel room door. Mumbling complaints under my breath got off the bed walked to the door and opened it. To my pleasant surprise Natasha Shranko was standing at the door with a gentle smile across her face. "I wondered how long it would take for you to get here," was her greeting as she pushed her way into my room. Typical Natasha is more forceful than waiting for invitations.

Walking to the table in the kitchenette she unrolled an old scroll she had under her arm. She said, "I know you are looking for clues to the symbol Sabastian the world president sent you to find." I asked, "how do you know that?"

she replied, "he told me he forcefully volunteered you for this adventure." Now I was a bit confused Natasha never and I mean never took on projects from anyone in a position of authority. She was one of those random situations never planned or expected. She had her own agenda and would show up after you did most of the research and relieve you of your prize. Besides the martial arts she had a regiment workout schedule.

"Sabastian offered me unlimited financial resources and people to find the treasure at the end of the rainbow so to speak." I came across an older woman called Mely in the mountain area above this city. Told her what I was looking for and she went into the back room with multiple locks and took out this scroll.

She gave it to me and said, "I knew you would show up in my lifetime. The prophecy declared a protector would show up requesting information about the symbolic metal icon and the holder of the scroll was to give her the scroll with these instructions. Find the boxes and inside each box is a symbol explained that all put together opens the symbolic icon the world president has. Keep the pieces and do not let the world president have it. Put them together and you will reveal a destiny for humankind that will cause the one world order to quake with fear."

That statement from Natasha sparked my curiosity and I rushed to the table to view the scroll. THE SCROLL HAD FIVE COLORS LISTED

1.RED

2.ORANGE

3.GREEN

4.BLUE

# 5.GOLD

Then a picture of a peculiar box with gears of some sort.

Natasha replied to my smile looking at the information on the scroll. "I knew you would have more of an idea about this as this is your area of research, so I asked Sabastian to send you but not to fill you in on what I found. I knew too much information would cause you to lose interest, so we positioned a few people along your path to speak mysteries to you and stare and whisper. This sparked your curiosity which guaranteed your arrival."

I turned to Natasha and said, "I guess you know me very well. Shall we get started?" She said, "where shall we start sweetheart?" She never called me sweetheart, so I was wondering if all our adventures together I made an imprint on her heart the same way she did to mine.

"Not sure Natasha, let's look at the image of the plaque again maybe we can find a starting point."

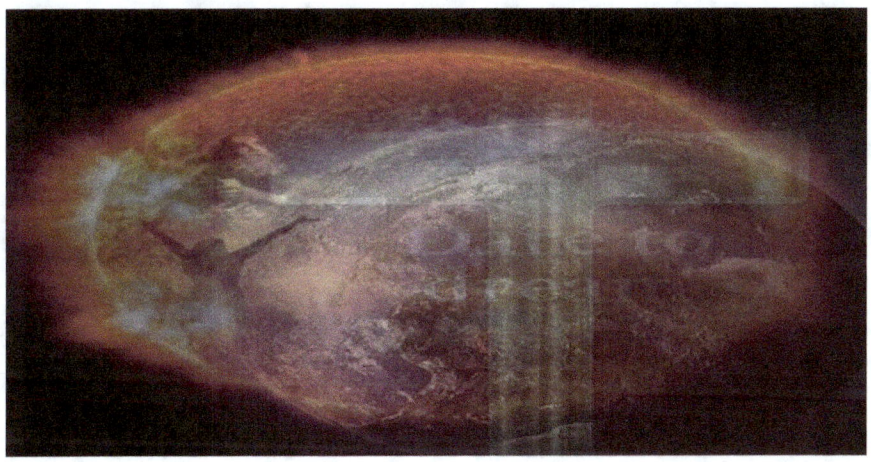

Natasha responded, "of all the images visible the words dare to dream are calling to me. Why not start with that?" "We have five color boxes to match, so how do we know what color to start with first," I responded. "Okay let's get a better understanding of the word dream," says Natasha.

She continued, "dreams are messy, some people think they have supernatural guidance through dreams while others think chemical reaction over foods ate. They could also represent goals, agendas, and purposes of individuals. Perchance what this is saying is we need wisdom to know what your soul or subconscious mind is trying to reveal to you?"

"Interesting" said Jack Roberts, "wisdom and tranquility in many cultures is represented by the color blue and blue is the fourth box listed. I think that is where we begin this expedition. What country and culture are best known for wisdom knowing how to apply the knowledge they have acquired over the years?" Natasha without hesitation said, "Israel, since they returned to their ancient land, they through their influence have turned the middle east into a paradise that feeds most of the world and the worlds technology wouldn't be as advanced  without the genius of Israel scientists and researchers." Since we had unlimited finances from the world president Natasha, and I decided to take a private jet to Israel rather than a commercial flight.

Upon arrival we were greeted in the airport by a rather unsure tour guide offering tours of excitement and adventure of the middle east and Israel. As exciting as he made it sound, we were not interested in tourist traps but off the grid adventures and made our thoughts to him noticeably clear and obvious to him. He grinned and said, "then I am your man and for ten percent of your profits I will show you places only spoken of in legends."

"We are not into selling any discoveries but collectors of ancient artifacts and if we give you five thousand American dollars will you show us these areas," responded Natasha.

The guide responded, "with pleasure," with a look of deception on his face. I intuitively knew we were about to be tourists trapped with fantastic stories created for gullible people. Regardless of the guide's agenda we fit into the whole travelers on vacation seeing the sites situation which would be a perfect cover so as to not be bothered by snoopy people.

The next few days were spent visiting local tourist sites in Israel that were in travel brochures, and his stories were so outrages of portals opening and aliens leaving gemstones behind with secret messages. He would use an ancient scroll discovered in Ethiopia as his source of information, the book of Enoch. I chuckled as I had read the book of Enoch and it is fascinating as it talks about creatures that fell from the heavens, mingled with humankind, and created a race  of beings different from both species.

This new race were giants with ferocious appetites and devoured everything in their path, all animals, hid in a mountain area in Lebanon.

These few people male and female were so well hidden the giants could never find them so turned on themselves to feed their appetites and cannibalized themselves out of extinction.

Natasha and I chuckled and thanked the guide for his great adventures and service well done. We parted company and decided to rent a two-bedroom house for a few months to explore surrounding countries on our own. After all we had unlimited expense account thanks to the world president Sabastian Hicks. We discussed the guides made up stories knowing every lie and fabrication has an element of truth which the lie uses to create its fantastic tale of greatness.

Deciding Lebanon would be an interesting place to visit we decided to see what information we could find on the internet about mount Petra.

Petra (Arabic:  Romanized: Al-Batra; Ancient Greek:  "Rock", Nabataean originally known to its inhabitants as Raqmu or Raqēmō, is an historic and archaeological city in southern Jordan. It is adjacent to the mountain of Jabal Al-Madbah, in a basin surrounded by mountains forming the eastern flank of the Arabah valley running from the Dead Sea to the Gulf of Aqaba. The area around Petra has been inhabited from as early as seven thousand BC, and the Nabataeans might have settled in what would become the capital city of their kingdom as early as the fourth century BC.

Archaeological work has only discovered evidence of Nabataean presence dating back to the second century BC, by which time Petra had become their capital.

The Nabataeans were nomadic Arabs who invested in Petra's proximity to the incense trade routes by establishing it as a major regional trading hub. Of the area's mountainous terrain. They were particularly skillful in harvesting rainwater, agriculture, and stone carving.

Petra flourished in the first century AD, when its Al-Khazneh structure – believed to be the mausoleum of Nabataean king Aretas IV – was constructed, and its population peaked at an estimated twenty thousand inhabitants. Although the Nabataean kingdom became a client state of the Roman Empire in the first century BC, it was only in one hundred six AD that it lost its independence. Petra fell to the Romans, who annexed Nabataea and renamed it as Arabia Petraea. Petra's importance declined as sea trade routes emerged, and after an earthquake in three sixty-three ad destroyed many structures.

In the Byzantine era several Christian churches were built, but the city continued to decline, and by the early Islamic era it was abandoned except for a handful of nomads. It remained unknown to the western world until eighteen twelve when Swiss traveler Johann Ludwig Burckhardt discovered it. Access to the city is through a 1.2-kilometre-long gorge called the Siq, which leads directly to the Khazneh. Famous for its rock-cut architecture and water conduit system, Petra is also called the "Rose City" because of the color of the stone from which it is carved. It has been a UNESCO World Heritage Site since 1985. UNESCO has described Petra as "one of the most precious cultural properties of man's cultural heritage."

In 2007, Al-Khazneh was voted one of the New 7 Wonders of the World.

Petra is a symbol of Jordan, as well as Jordan's most-visited tourist attraction. Tourist numbers peaked at 1.1 million in 2019, marking the first time that the figure rose above the one million marks. Tourism in the city was crippled by the COVID-19 pandemic, but soon after started to pick up again, reaching 905,000 visitors in 2022.

Interesting enough, the caves burrowed into the side of the mountain enticed me. Did they go anywhere or were they cut into the rock as a dwelling place for individual families and only one way in no exit or back door to escape in case front entrance was blocked? Time to find out.

# THE BLUE BOX

Natasha and I agreed to create a back story for our expedition. We were a newly married couple on our honeymoon seeing the wonders of the world. Our first stop was the city built into the side of a mountain. Mount Petra was an exciting tourist adventure according to the brochures. The first few days were exploring multiple caves that were no more than dwellings with no way in or out except the entrance. A quick look around was all that was needed to see nothing of interest except mayb4e a piece of broken pottery from a squabble between a couple where she got mad at him and through a vase at his back as he was leaving the dwelling to avoid  big time confrontation.

Getting tired and beginning to think this was a waste of time, we entered a cave of interest. There were markings in a language unfamiliar to us,

"שער השמים" (Sha'ar HaShamayim)." and upon querying our new  guide, she responded that the message was the entrance to  heaven was the words over the entrance to what seemed a back door or entrance to another  dwelling place. I asked has anyone explored that area and she said, "Yes but only leads to a pool of water and goes no further. She summarized that maybe that pool was a hot spring at one time and people used it as a span and got much needed relaxation and comfort to the body thus calling it the entrance to "heaven." Natasha thanked her and gave me a knowing smile; we were coming back after hours to do our own expedition of the pool area.

The tour was over, so we quickly sought out a scuba diving shop to purchase equipment for an underwater adventure. Later that night we made our way back to the cave with the entrance to heaven marking and went inside to the  pool. Our flashlights were not super bright to attract attention but just enough to be able to see a couple of feet ahead of us.

After we passed through the entrance to heaven doorway, we walked for about one quarter of a mile descending at a fifteen degrees slope. We finally came to a large opening that could hold about twenty people comfortably. In the center of this area was a  pool of water that was clear. The pool never showed a bottom, so you knew it was a natural phenomenon and not man made. Quickly getting our equipment on, we prepared for what we hoped would be a successful dive. Underwater scuba diving was something we had done on many occasions looking for treasures of various sorts. Assessing the water before we lowered ourselves in, we realized it was lukewarm and not icy cold much to our thankfulness.

We lowered ourselves into the pool and began swimming to each of the sides to explore for the entrance where the water came in. The pool is only twenty feet wide and was easy to check, left and right sides only finding rock. The end of the pool was about sixty feet away. We swam to the end and found what seemed to be a six-foot-in-diameter entrance into the wall. Motioning Natasha to follow me, I entered the tunnel. We swam for what seemed an hour and suddenly a yellowish light seemed to shine through the clear water. The tunnel continued but we wanted to explore the light and ascend to the surface.

Near the surface we discovered a gold plate that covered the exit to the tunnel. The gold plate was illuminating a yellowish gold color light which both Natasha and I Jack found quite appealing and, being inquisitive by nature, we wanted to know the reason for such illumination.

We began pressing on the plate to hopefully find a button or switch that would cause the plate to move and reveal an exit from the water. Searching for twenty minutes we found what seemed like a handle on the rock wall and pushed it up. The water started to get turbulent as the gold plate began to move and a ladder started to descend into the water. Enough of the gold plate moved to create an exit and the ladder stopped with the bottom about three in the water making it easier to exit rather than pulling ourselves up rung by rung until we could get our feet under us on a rung of the ladder.

Our instruments on our wrist showed a breathable atmosphere so we turned off our oxygen tanks saving air for the trip back. We decided to keep our equipment on even though it was a bit of an inconvenience to explore in scuba gear, but we didn't want to leave our equipment on a moving plate but on stationary ground so as to return to this area and find the gold covered plate moved totally off the water and dumped our equipment into the water and lost forever.

We climbed about sixty feet and discovered a room full of jewels, gold cups, parchments and different shaped articles piled together. I knew this was a distraction from what we were searching for.

Natasha's desire for shiny things would cause her to want to load up as much as she could carry and take with her back to the pool. As soon as she picked up a ruby from the table the ceiling started to lower at a quick pace. "Put it back, I said, "the table is a pressure switch as soon as the weight changes then ceiling will drop crushing everything in the room."

Natasha replaced the ruby and the ceiling stopped but never went back up. Natasha looking around at the items on the table said, "I guess we can search for the blue box by sliding the items around without lifting them, then how are we going to get the box off and survive if we find it?" "We will have to guess the weight of the box and try to find something exact to match it and replace it simultaneously ." said Jack. Slowly moving items across the table while not lifting them we found our blue box. It looked fourteen ounces to a pound, so I found a stone that weighed close to the box, so I thought.

I noticed Natasha picking up a few stones and I asked her :what are you doing?" she replied, "I can't take all the goodies but might as well try for a few that won't weigh me down while swimming back to heaven's gate pool." I knew better to argue with her. She got her stones and put the jewels she wanted together so as to make it easier and quicker. She placed them near the side of the table so she could slide them into the fanny pouch she was wearing while placing the stones on the table. I cleared the blue box away from other items so as to not accidently knock something off the table thus the weight difference causing the ceiling to come down. I said, "together on three we will make the switch, don't be greedy and take more because the ceiling will come down and crush everything making them valueless." Three two one the switch was made, and the ceiling of stone never moved, and we agreed to come back another time to see if we could not salvage more of the treasure, but for now keep it secret from other treasure hunters. We made our way back to our scuba gear where we left it on a flat rock that was stationary and not movable. Putting on our scuba gear we decided to try and close the gold metal covering when we left to prevent explorers from finding the entrance to the treasure. We  made it back to the gold plate covering, entered the water to notice it was a bit warmer, so we closed the gold covering and headed back to the heavens gate entrance. While swimming we noticed fish were turning belly up and dying because the water was too warm for them.

We noticed an underwater volcano in the distance that just became active. Getting out of the ocean was a priority as we did not want to boil in sea water. After a heated workout swimming as fast as we could we finally arrived at the pool in Heaven's gate cave. Now we would have to make it back to our room without being noticed. We arrived at Petra while it was dark and noticed the sun was starting to rise. We were active all night on this expedition and hoped it was worth the time. Once we got back to our two-bedroom suite we would rest then check out our salvaged treasure and see if it was an excellent payday.

After ten hours sleep, we put our treasure on the table and looked intently at the blue box. The jewels Natasha took did not interest me as she would find an appraiser, get quotes and sell them anyway. This man Jack Roberts was more interested in solving the puzzle of the symbol and see where it leads.

After playing with the gears or dials we figured out that it was a combination lock and to get the right sequence would allow the box to be opened. We started at the top and began turning the gears and they just spun freely with nonresistance. Nothing happened or a different sound, so we proceeded to the next set of dials and did the same thing and nothing again. When we went to the right side of the box and began turning the dials, we could hear a slight clicking noise then suddenly a loud clack and the dial would move no more.

We summarized that the dials on the side should be first part of the combination then the top to lift the lid and see what the contents of the box are. Thinking it was a combination lock we started turning the dial on the left side opposite to how we turned the dial on the right side and success. The dial started clicking quietly then a loud sounding clack then the dial would not turn anymore. Natasha, being impulsive, could not wait so she started turning the dial the same way  as the right side and suddenly a clack and boom the sides of the box fell open while the lid covered the contents of the box. I lifted the lid to  reveal two items, a square looking object and a picture.

The square item looked like a computer processor. The top of the processor had the same symbol we were trying to investigate, so obviously that individual or company developed it thereof. The picture seemed very general in its application because multiple religions have multiple gods, and which one do you want to emulate? We decided to send the world president the picture dare to dream like God simply because his thoughts of being deity will set him at ease thinking no one is against him. If he thinks this is a message from the invisible realm telling humankind to dream like him because he is god then all should be at peace in his mind.

# THE RED BOX

Natasha and I knew a man on the west coast who could separate merged pictures once he had the picture thus leaving it clearer to view. According to Mely from the Philippines we had to find five boxes which represented the five pictures merged into one to create the symbol on the iron plate found by the world president's agents. We had one picture clue (dare to dream God's dream), and if we could separate that from the others that might make it easier to view other pictures to get an idea where to go next.

Our friend photo shop perry got his nickname from doing much photo shopping for people who wanted to avoid corrupt government agents. He kept his real name on the down low  as to not attract attention from the one world president who he was not a fan of and enjoyed helping people resist his policies and agendas which were self-serving.

Upon arrival in Chilliwack, a government agent confronted us, "Jack, Natasha president

Sabastian thanks you for the first clue. He was pleased that it was about people following and adapting not his dreams and goals for humanity.

I smiled at Natasha while telling the agent to tell the world president we were pleased to serve him. Keeping the world president off balance and in the dark to what is taking place was the only way to see this mission fulfilled. The world president thinking it was a mission for his exaltation when it was a mission to dethrone him.

Photoshop perry separated the picture dare to dream God's dream from the image symbol and a cross with a dove sitting on the left side of the cross beam appeared more clearly than before.

Talking it over with Natasha we both agreed the cross with the dove should be our next adventure. We concluded this adventure was to immerse ourselves in the one world religion that was currently controlling the earth now. All other religions have compromised their ideals and dogmas to keep peace until the current religious bully on the block could be removed.

No matter how you look at religion, from a negative or positive perspective, bondage to its tenants, Rules, traditions, and regulations have always kept humanity in bondage. This kind of bondage blinds the participants from seeing what is actually happening in life. There is freedom in relationships which is desired by most civilians of the earth. Religious concepts seek to  elevate individuals over others and make self-exalted ones famous and the focus of others to be idolized and deemed greater than all within their sphere  of influence.

Our next adventure would take us to the city on seven hills where the religious temple was built on the ancient catacombs. These catacombs were secret meeting places for religions that were being persecuted in the first century. These catacombs went on for miles with secret caves which were used as burial places where treasures were hidden in the graves. No one thought people would contaminate themselves by digging into graves of rotted flesh for some treasures that were rumored to be just a trinket that was only valuable to the individual being buried but no value in the world system at that time.

Natasha and I agreed to get access to the catacombs, we could not resent ourselves as tourists but rather clergy of the one world church. The one world church was a rather strange entity. It publicly acknowledged the world president and his supposed deity while plotting to take over the world system. Seems like anybody in a position of authority had ideas of grandeur to control humanity for their own agendas. Most world dictator wannabes think their goals, plans and agendas are best for civilians who in their mind do not actually know what they want and cannot see the need of.

These are the fantasies of self-deluded people who think they know what is best for others. Regardless of other's plans and desires we need to find the red box. Natasha scrummaged through a closet and found a couple of uniforms that conveniently our size and we blended in with the leadership of the religious order.

We began to mingle with others in uniform asking questions. I noticed Natasha leaving with a burly mam in a different uniform. She put on the facade of a struggle to make people think she was being apprehended for some violations. A little verbal complaining, and she was ushered through an entrance. Just before the door closed, she turned her face toward me and smiled and winked.

I chuckled to myself, knowing that even this person was twice her size and by outward appearance Natasha would be at his mercy, which was not the case. Natasha was going to question or should I say interrogate this person for information leading to the catacombs. This agent thought he was interrogating Natasha, and she was playing along manipulating him to answer her questions and get the answers she desired. I waited for about ten minutes then excused myself from the others.

I snuck over to the entrance where Natasha and the large agent disappeared through and slowly made my way to the area where the agent was supposedly interrogating Natasha. I stayed in the shadows watching the agent slap my love around asking her who she worked for and what her plans were. She would respond by asking him a question totally infuriating him. I had to resist the temptation to rush to her aid knowing she was in control even though it looked like she was being abused and beaten.

In frustration the agent gave Natasha the information she wanted. He thought he was in control and going to end her life as soon as he was done questioning her. The agent pulled a gun from his holster and pointed it at Natasha and said, "last chance to spill the information I want." Natasha responded, "I got what I want and thank you so now I am done with you." The agent looked puzzled wondering what she was talking about, done with me? She was the one tied up in the chair and being beaten by him! Little did the agent know that while he was slapping her around, she was freeing herself from her ropes. Natasha is an excellent escape artist and has been on many missions that require that talent.

She stood to her feet at the surprise of the agent and a little jujitsu here Kungfu there and a touch of kick boxing and the agent was lying on the floor being tied up with his own ropes by Natasha.

She noticed me in the shadows and said, "glad you didn't interfere with my interrogation session."

Talk about a tough female, don't be mean to her or you will be regretting it. She looked at me and said, "follow me I know how to get to the catacombs." I followed Natasha out of the temple to a cave on the side of a mountain and thought "what is it about caves and treasures?" we entered the cave and after a couple of turns down some adjoining tunnels we headed back to the direction of the temple just underground. After about an hour of spelunking through tunnels under ground we entered a large area where we noticed the walls have been dug into and bodies, or shall I say skeletons remained. I was smart to drop markers along the way; I didn't want to get lost in the maze of tunnels we traversed.

We used our high-end spelunkers light to illuminate each grave site to see what's in there. Didn't want to stick our hands in each grave in the dark and feel around, don't know what kind of critter is in there. After about a dozen graves, we found the red box in a grave with a glass plate in front of it.

Now to the Squamish this wouldn't happen. I had to move the skeleton out of the way to remove the glass plate from in front of the red box to retrieve it. I say gently because like the blue box there could be booby traps.

I ,Jack, slowly and cautiously moved the skeleton expecting something to happen but much to my relief the walls and ceiling didn't move. The glass plate was a bit tough to move but I decided to give it a good push to force it out of the way.  The glass plate moved enough to grab the red box and a trap door opened above the red box. Not a fan of snakes, I closed my eyes after putting on shoulder length gloves and reached in to grab the box. Snakes began striking the gloves but were unable to penetrate the material to inflict harm on myself. Retrieving the red box, we followed our markers out of the tunnels to the entrance to the cave.

We decided not to open the box in that area not knowing what to expect but retired to our hotel room in that city. In our room we went through the combinations again and the box fell open and revealed the picture and a note.

The note said revelation of covenant. This must not be known, or control will be lost.

Now that presented a mystery in itself. Why would covenant cause a loss of control? Perchance the mystery would be solved after all the pieces were put together. Now to go see photo shop Perry and let him do his magic.

# THE GREEN BOX

After photoshop Perry removed the cross and dove from the other pictures, this is what remained.

Even though you could see the figure of an older man in the background the picture of the earth stood out more than others. Natasha and I Jack  concluded the next clue had to do with living things on the earth. Being anxious to continue our search for clues I asked Natasha, "the earth is a big place, any idea where we might start looking?" I was surprised at Natasha's answer. "Jack sweetheart we need a vacation. We have been through a lot of stress, danger, excitement, and other physical draining activities. The other boxes aren't going anywhere. The first two boxes were hidden quite well and protected by booby traps so I am sure the last three will be as well. I was surprised and pleased she called me sweetheart. Usually, she is tough and emotionless like she was with the agent who thought he was interrogating her but was being manipulated by her for info9rmation. I smiled, danced, and jumped for joy on the inside. I was seeing a softer side of the woman I fell in love with over the course of this adventure. She called me sweetheart, maybe her heart was getting tender towards me so I will play it out to the max in order to see her motives, agendas, and purposes. "yes, Natasha you are right, we need rest, relaxation." Before I could get another word from my lips, she pulled me close to her and said "ROMANCE" and planted the most passionate kiss on me ever. "Jack, I have been in love with you for years but have never felt you thought the same way until I noticed you restraining yourself from doing the chivalrous thing most men would jump at to impress me when the agent was slapping me around. You knew me and understood my way of thinking and it takes love to resist trying to impress me for your own personal feelings. That's when I knew you loved me." "yes, Natasha, I do love you and want to spend every adventure from here on until our greatest adventure will be waking up first in order to beat the other one to the bathroom."

She giggles and says, " I always wanted to visit the space city station revolving around the earth. I have never been there and heard it was a place of beauty and peace away from the influence of the world president and his no choice policies." I agreed. "since the world president has given you unlimited financial sources, surely we can use some for a vacation but tell the world president our next clue is out of this world." "Done" said Natasha, "I will make the arrangements and book the tickets for the shuttle upwards and beyond." I thanked Natasha for her kindness while thinking who names these shuttles to sp0ace city and other colonized planets, we have put mankind on?

The year is twenty-six seven hundred-forty cycles, and you would think we would come up with something better, but that is mankind, smart in some areas, but not so in others. I was looking to spending time with Natasha where our focus was on each other and nothing else. I prematurely  thought that was Natashas desire as well but who can figure out women was the old man's dilemma in ancient times but still true in the future.

We were standing in the boarding line for the shuttle when a government agent approached Natasha and I and said here are your tickets and the president says hopefully you will find what you are looking for, most people are blind about the clues you sent back to us, it seems to be beyond their comprehension.

Natasha accepted the tickets, and we boarded the shuttle craft to space city when she turned to me and said, "hope you didn't hear what the government agent said but I know you well. After a couple of days relaxing romance and rest you will get restless and want to start the mission again."

I responded, "so true, you got me all figured out." Natasha continued, "besides the earth I could see the picture of the sun as well. You missed it didn't you?" hmm I guess I did; you always were sharper than me, that's why we make a good team. You are the brains and the combat expert, and I lift the heavy boxes. Natasha not wanting me to feel dumb around her graciously said, "you figured out many things I missed in the past, so you are pretty intelligent as well, and yes we make a great team." "Anyways that told me our next clues would be out of the atmosphere of the earth where we could view the earth surface as we revolved around it and could see the sun, so naturally space city was the place to look," Natasha continued. "Makes total sense sweety," Jack replied. "Then once those clues are figured out, we can hopefully understand the figure of the man and its relevance to the complete puzzle and  the world president's concerns, anticipation and confusion about the original symbol his agents discovered." Natasha said, "as long as we keep the world president thinking it is still about his glorification to godhood and the citizen of the earth agrees with him then we will be safe to pursue this mission with our motives in mind."

Leaving the spaceport runway was smooth but we exp0eriebnced a little turbulence as we ascended to the upper atmosphere. My window seat was extraordinary as I watched the clouds disappear. The  atmosphere of earth is divided into four layers; troposphere, stratosphere, mesosphere, and thermosphere, going through each layer was a sight to see and remember.

Suddenly we were in the blackness of space and the pilot over the speaker system gave the passengers the usual tourist speech. "Hope you enjoyed your ascent through the earth's atmosphere, and you will experience a moment of weightlessness until we get the gravity plating set properly. Please keep your seat belts on for your safety. Once the seat belt light goes out you are free to get up, walk around and go to our dining room for a meal. It will be about an eight-hour flight to space city. Thank you for your patience. The shuttle crafts that took us to space city and the colonized planets were not small.

They each had ten decks and personal quarters for each family or individual. Total passenger capacity worked out to be five thousand people besides ship's crew and employees for passenger comforts such as dining and room maintenance. A complete medical staff was present on each shuttle craft for those unforeseen circumstances that always play gottcha. Each passenger was treated with honor, dignity and respect simply because this was a luxury tour to space city where the marvels never cease to amaze visitors.

The fasten seatbelt sign went out and a stewardess spoke over the microphone and stated we have now started your space flight to our destination. You are free to move about the shuttle and go to your assigned cabins and enjoy our dining restaurants.

The initial departure from the earth's atmosphere required all passengers to sit in a common area where they were seat belted in their seats because the earth's atmosphere could get turbulent as we passed through it into space. Natasha and I left the communal area and found a classy dining restaurant to relax and enjoy a quiet romantic meal.

Eventually we found a concierge to show us to our assigned cabins where we could rest and have a nap until we arrived at space city. In our room there were two double beds for our complete comfort, which I enjoyed because I toss and turn and take up the whole bed.

Natasha would use the other bed and get some sleep. After a few hours' rest we were awakened by a ship wide announcement for all travelers to go to the common area because we are twenty minutes away from landing procedures to space city. Brush my teeth, a wash of my face, kiss Natasha on the forehead and we were on our way to the common area to prepare for landing procedures to space city. Landing was smooth and uneventful.

We were greeted by a baggage handler who took our luggage and showed us to our reserved quarters that had been supplied to us by the world president. Upon entrance we tipped the baggage handler and closed the door without saying a word.

I wrote a note to Natasha saying, THE WORLD PRESIDENT SUPPLIED THE ROOM SO IT'S PROBABLY BUGGED WITH LISTENING DEVICES, SO WE HAVE TO ACT THE PART OF WORKING FOR HIM.

She nodded, then we unpacked our luggage and began to act out the parts we rehearsed in our quarters on the shuttle craft. After about an hour's performance to satisfy any listeners, we decided to leave the room and explore space city.

Leaving our room, we took the elevator to the main floor of the hotel, and we were greeted by a tour guide. He explained his services were prepaid for a few days so ask him anything we want; he would take us anywhere we wanted to go. So, we played the part of interested tourists and asked the size of the city and how it operates and stays active. He informed us of the size, seventy-five miles in circumference, with oxygen stations to generate breathable atmosphere every ten miles. They are maintained on a regular basis and have priority over all maintenance schedules. He explained the water creation process to help irrigate the farmland of super soil that can grow ten crops of eatable food each cycle. Then he started on the museums and ancient artifacts they discovered on the colonized planets. The museums caught our attention.

We spent the next two days letting the tour guide take us to the five museums in the city. We explored each museum thoroughly searching for clues to the green box. Not finding anything, we were tempted to  start looking in corn fields or cow pastures for an **X that marks the spot for buried treasure.** The tour guide mentioned one more museum that we might find interesting, it is called Mishkin museum. Apparently, the artifacts on display here have been discovered entering the outer regions of our solar system from somewhere beyond our known existence. It's like someone sent these artifacts here to tease, tempt, or somehow reveal himself in some unique way. Now that statement caused us to stand at attention.

The tour guide agreed to take us to this museum in the morning as it was now closed and getting late. Time for dinner, dancing and a night of entertainment which Natasha and I needed to relax and rest. With anticipation and excitement, we retired for the night hopeful that we would discover clues to the green box. Waking in the morning Natasha looked at me and said, :hopefully we are done with caves and tunnels. I would like the other boxes to be not so physically challenging.

Mind scramblers I can deal with but the whole work physically gets tiring after a while. Natasha got what she wished for, upon entering the Mishkin museum the curator showed us his prize artifacts which included a green box with gears.

The pure gold, pure rubies and other unflawed jewels were protected by laser beams that would dismember you if you tried to steal them and since Natasha had enough shiny things to last her a lifetime, she resisted the temptation for more. Besides, penalties for crime were extreme in space cities.

We asked about the green box and the curator said, "it's an interesting item. It has no apparent value but when it was discovered on planet Sol Tar in the outer region it was embedded with this contraption in the center of each side. We tried to remove it, but it stays firm. We tried to physically remove it to inspect it, but electric shocks are generated each time a physical application is applied. We noticed it is in the center so we thought there might be two boxes like it that might be a clue to open the box or release it from the contraption.

We asked the curator if we could come back after hours and show him something that might help solve the puzzle of the green box. He agreed and set a time when we could sit with him without the scrutiny of the tour guide.

We went back to our room and did an impressive performance for anyone who might be listening. We talked about how the museums were fruitless and we should go explore the more rural areas of space city. A few hours later we decided to meet the curator. We packed our other two boxes with us, and they even passed inspection because to the officers they didn't fall under contraband and looked harmless.

Upon arrival at the museum the curator let us in and locked the door behind us. He then turned to  us and asked, 'are you for or against the world president and the world religion leader?" Natasha responded, "I am working for him on a mission and Jack is working for me, but we are not fans of either entity." The curator responded, "good, the citizens of space city live here because they are tired of the manipulation on planet earth and desire a lifestyle of freedom and choices. If you were for him, I would have asked you to leave because no one in space city trusts him, and his agents who try to infiltrate our city are sent back to earth. We have a defense system against any kind of attack from the earth and beyond. Not only that we are so far from the earth it's not worth the worlds president to be overly concerned on any influence we might have on his empire," continued the curator.

All of us wandered over to the stand where the green box sat in its contraption. We took out the other two boxes and showed them to the curator. He was amazed and stated he never knew about those boxes and wanted an explanation. We shared how we arrived at the need of the five boxes to solve the symbol on the metal plate that the world president's agents discovered. Since Natasha and I were the worlds most prominent research and puzzle solving people, we were hired to discover the meaning of the symbol on the metal plate and if it affected his empire in any way?

After showing him, the boxes and pictures removed from the metal plate and the processor, he smiled a knowing smile. Natasha looked at the contraption in the middle of the green box and asked, "what order do these other boxes fit into the holes." The curator said, "put them in according to the order you found them from left to right." "Jack, you do it," said Natasha. I put them in and was pleased that an orange light began to illuminate and the gears on the green box began to move and fall into place unlocking the box. We had unlocked the other boxes previously, so the green box was unlocked when inserted.

We later discovered upon examining the contraption and discovered instructions in symbolic form that read if the blue and red boxes were inserted while locked, they would trigger an explosion that would destroy all boxes, and the knowledge would be lost forever, and mankind would be subject to evil empires for all eternity.

We put the pictures and notes discovered in each box side by side and got an encouraging but cryptic message

1. Blue box- dare to dream god's dream
2. Red box-revelation of covenant
3. green box-you have the right, power, and ability to make choices

The curator smiled and said, "the orange box is your next adventure. I don't think that box is going to be found on earth but on one of the colonies in the outer regions since the green box was discovered out there coming from a trajectory beyond our solar system."

Both Natasha and I agreed with the curator. He offered us a small crate which we could put all our discovered artifacts in, including the green box which he documented to give us for a collection piece to our material valueless collection of boxes. This would throw off any agents or crooks thinking we were some fanatical types collecting useless boxes. Perfect, now to research the museum curator's database to find a colonized planet in the outer

regions of our solar system to look for the last
two boxes.

# THE ORANGE BOX

Orange in most cultures represents caution, potential danger approaching. So , turning to Natasha I asked, "how long do you want to stay in space city before we go looking for the next clue?

Natasha replied, "I found a planet that was discovered a few centuries ago and a question that was asked caused the building of a exon space craft that can hold ten thousand people and enough supplies for ten years to start the colonization of the planet. The planet was in the constellation cygnus. Here is what I found in the museum database."

Kepler-452b is a super Earth exoplanet orbiting within the inner edge of the habitable zone of the sun like star Kepler-452 and is the only planet in the system discovered by the Kepler telescope. It is located about eighteen hundred light years away from earth in the constellation Cygnus.

Can humans live on Kepler 452b? astronomers say that the planet is in the "goldilocks zone," meaning that the distance of the planet from the star is just right, making it not to hot and not to cold for human life to exist.

The world organization chose genetically healthy people who volunteered for the adventure of colonization of the planet. They were made aware of the hardships and potential dangers of the unknown. They had enough fuel to make multiple round trips.

"Since our ability to travel through space quickly with the discovery of bending in the form of worm holes we can get anywhere in another solar system within a few hours," said Natasha.

The museum curator excused his interruption and said, "there is a Xeon ship making a supply run in a week and I will see if I can book you passage on the ship. These Xeon ships are slowly becoming passenger cruise ships for people who want to visit the planet.

The original colonizers did a tremendous job of establishing of establishing colonies on that world and cities are being built at an extraordinary rate and trading minerals, metals, and other various products has become a new industry standard."

Natasha looked at me and said, "as soon as our tickets are secure, I will make a request, suggestion, demand on the earth president that we discovered another clue on Kepler 452b that could solve the puzzle and secure his desire for godhood," she grinned and winked at me as she said this. We both knew she was just feeding an overinflated ego to secure our safe trip without interference from agents. One week later two envelopes arrived at the door of our hotel room. The tickets for our trip and a letter from the world president. The letter reads you have my authority to travel to that planet but be careful, I have no agents to watch over you there and no authority or influence there in any sense of the word. You will be on your own.

We were given image of Kepler 452b compared to earth and looked like an interesting planet to search for clues.

Natash and I entered the space port and were met by two burly government agents who said nervously, "don't think you can get away from our scrutiny, we have secret agents in every known solar system, we are always watching." I chuckled and turned to Natasha and said, "we better be on our best behavior, or these mean agents might spank our bottoms." Natasha grinned and lunged towards one of the agents and he jerked back remembering the beating Natasha gave him a while back. Then she said, "this should be fun."

Boarding the Xeon ship was uneventful, and we found our seats and strapped ourselves in to enjoy our space flight. Natasha fell asleep and I grabbed a tourist pamphlet of the planet and spent a couple of minutes reading it, then engaged in conversation with a man in an adjoining seat. This man had made the journey between planets and was bringing his family to the new colony as he built their home and established his trading business. Little did I realize this trader would be helpful in finding the orange box. After a couple of hours, the pilot declared our arrival. We traversed eighteens hundred light years in two hours.

Leaving the Xeon ship we looked for a hotel or cabin to rent until we could find a more suitable place to live. We spent two months exploring the planet and soon Natasha and I agreed we could settle down together and live on Kepler 452b.

To buy a home or better yet built according to your specifications and desires was cheap. Natasha and I took work as explorers of the planet to help people find new areas to build cities and we were paid extremely well. We cut ourselves off from the earth dwellers and their religious and political systems. It was time to continue our mission to find the boxes and solve the symbol on the metal plate discovered by government agents.

We began asking questions and were pleasantly surprised that we never ran into a mean or cantankerous person. The city of andromeda where we took residence was located on the shores of a large lake in a tropical paradise where an abundance of fruit was grown to feed the other colonies on this planet.

There was no ill will amongst the colonies. They shared each other's resources for the well-being and benefit of each colony. There was no desire for competition for profit or financial gain as the economic system was not built around acquired wealth and power to live luxuriously and be exalted above other people. All citizens of the planet were considered equal and a desire to share and serve each other was promoted on the planet as per the constitution of the planet. For some reason, this new way of life flourished and any desire to be like earth dwellers was quickly forgotten.

A new planet, a new way to live. After months of searching for clues to the orange box we hit every dead end you could think of and just  decided to rest for a bit to get our minds off the puzzle. Natasha and I decided to go to the beach for an afternoon suntan. The weather was sunny and very warm but not too hot to burn and be uncomfortable.

As evening was setting in, we decided to go home when the trader we had met on the Xeon ship approached us. "Jack, Natasha I have something to show you that might help your quest for five boxes to solve the symbol found embedded in the metal plate on earth by the government agents." Jack responded, "how do you know about the symbol?" The  trader said "who do you think sent it to earth as a warning for the religious and political orders and hope for the common civilians. The people of our planet f9ound a book that speaks of a momentous event coming to the planet earth and we thought earth needed a heads-up message. We figured if we did through symbolism people would be curious enough to search it out. We realized that if we declared it publicly the religious community would stop it in its tracks." Natasha's curiosity was spiked, "let's go Jack I need to see this." We arrived at our home, and the trader went to his vehicle and brought into our house a medium-sized box of oranges and placed them on the cupboard. A letter was on top titled THE FRUIT OF THE SPIRIT.

He said, "you thought you were looking for an orange- colored box with a combination like the other three you found. Not every puzzle piece is the same. Let us look at what you discovered so far."

One. The blue box with the processor

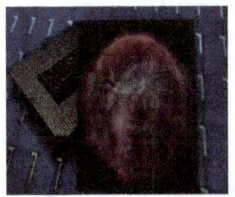

and the picture

Two. The red box with the pictures

three. The green box: you have the right, power, and ability to make choices

four: box of oranges with the letter fruit of the spirit. We opened the letter and it read, "Galatians  five verses twenty-two through twenty-six, but the fruit of the Spirit is love, joy, peace, longsuffering, kindness, goodness, faithfulness, gentleness, self-control. Against such there is no law, and those who are Christs have crucified the flesh with its passions and desires. If we live in the Spirit, let us also walk in the spirit. Let us not become conceited, provoking one another, envying one another."

The trader explained that each of these boxes and contents including the fruit of oranges had its origin from someone outside the human race which was the answer to the fifth box and the picture of the older man.

# THE GOLD BOX

Natasha and I thanked the trader for his help as it was invaluable. We were so close to solving the symbol, realizing the magnitude of its meaning. The answer rested in the gold box and what it contained.

Where to look was a mystery and both Natasha and I agreed we could search for a long time thinking one thing and be misinformed like the orange box. We had our minds set that all the clues were exactly the same but changed with the fourth box. Maybe the fifth and final gold box was not the same as the first three but like the fourth box different in its application and approach.

After a couple of months asking questions about a gold box, we ended up in an old timer's tech shop. He built electronic items like main boards for computers, circuit boards and other electronic items that enticed people. We asked him if he knew off hand of a gold box with gears that were actually combinations that would open the box? He chuckled and said, "the thing you are looking for was dropped off by a mysterious individual and asked if I would store it here for them until a couple came and asked for it according to the same statement you just made. I was paid handsomely to do that so why not. Wait here while I go to the closet and retrieve it.

The old timer came back and put the gold box on his work bench and asked, "if you know how to open the box would you mind if I watched and find out what I was paid to protect until you showed up?" Natasha said, "we would like that, who knows you might play a crucial part in the contents of the box, just saying." "thanks," responded the old timer. Jack started to turn the gears in the same manner as before but got nothing. Natasha said, "everything is different here try going backwards starting from the last gear we did on earth. So, jack went to the last and worked his way to the first and the box opened. The old timer laughed and said the parable is fulfilled today. Jack asked, "what parable?" the old timer pointed to a clay plaque hanging on his wall which read THE FIRST SHALL BE LAST AND THE LAST SHALL BE FIRST. He looked at my puzzled face and said, "it means equality, no one is greater than anyone else and all mankind are of equal value which is beyond measure."

"wow what a unique way of thinking. The only way most humanity knows, especially amongst religious and political leaders, is self-exaltation proclaiming their greatness above and beyond others," Natasha spoke strongly. "lets open this box and see the answer to our quest," Jack said.

Doing the combination from last to first caused the box to open and proved the saying everything is not the way it looks and is perceived to be by natural circumstances and information. The box opened and revealed a gold circuit main board and memory sticks.

The old technician said all we need is the
processor to fit and we have got a complete
working unit. I placed the processor we found
on the work bench. The technician smiled and
began to inspect the pieces and soon had them
assembled perfectly. "wow," he grinned this is
interesting. "I have a two-thousand-watt power
supply I can hook to this, and we will see what
happens when we turn this thing on. Hooking
the circuit board to his monitor and input and
output devices he hit the power switch and a
strange golden glow appeared on the ceiling. In
the middle of the glow was an image of an
older man.

And voices that sounded like trumpets spoke and said, **I AM THE ANCIENT OF DAYS AND MAKE JUDGMENTS CONCERNING THE SAINTS AND I AM RETURNING TO THE EARTH TO TAKE POSESSION OF WHAT IS RIGHTFULLY MINE SINCE I CREATED THE EARTH AND IT'S INHABITANTS. THE EARTH IS MINE AND THE FULLNESS THEREOF.**

The golden glow turned off and all went silent. The technician sat stunned then queried, " do you know how to find the revelatory one? Only he can give you the proper meaning to all your symbols, clues, and pictures, from the first glances I do not want to be the religious and political leaders of the earth, the future doesn't look to good for them."

Natasha turned to Jack asking, "do you know how to find the one who brings revelation so we can put this adventure to rest?"

## Take Refuge from the Coming Judgment

Come, my people, enter your chambers,
And shut your doors behind you;
Hide yourself, as it were, for a little moment,
Until the indignation is past.
For behold, the Lord comes out of His place
To punish the inhabitants of the earth for their iniquity;
The earth will also disclose her blood,
And will no more cover her slain.

# EPILOGUE

I choose to use this genre of science fiction to share  a point of view from the paradigm that I live in. from my perspective we can as earth dwellers under the slavery of political and religious dominance which only seeks to control and manipulate citizens of earth for their own agendas. Some religious groups even claim to be a move of God but eventually show their true colors of being a denominational empire seeking fame and wealth and world influence.

The alternate to being earth dwellers is to be citizens of heaven in covenant with the ancient of days. This citizenship gives us the right and ability to choose freely with the results of our choices being experienced by our selves and not having to be affected by the choices of others. The Holy Spirit is the one who brings revelation to your lifestyle and destiny. Man or woman, no matter the position of authority they claim to hold has the ability to reveal your destiny in Christ. Those that exalt themselves will be brought low.

Second Corinthians thirteen verse fourteen

New King James Version

The grace of the Lord Jesus Christ, and the love of God, and the communion of the Holy Spirit *be* with you all. Amen.

## ABOUT THE AUTHOR

William is a kind, considerate, compassionate man and enjoys writing as a hobby. Mostly he loves encouraging people to follow after the Holy Spirit who is the only one who can help each individual  to find their destinies.